SCOOBY-DOO!

MINIATURE GOLF
MYSTERY

Written by Matt Kelly
Illustrated by Vincent Musacchia
Digital color and production by Dwight Wanhala

Read along and follow Scooby and the gang on their
mysterious adventure! You will know it is time to turn
the page when you hear this sound.... Now, let's see what
Scooby, Shaggy, and the rest of the gang are up to!

The Mystery Machine is driving down a dark road on its way to
Coolsville. Scooby and the gang are restless and want to take a break.

"Like, are we there yet?" Shaggy asks.

As the Mystery Machine turns a corner, Fred spots a large sign.
"Look! A miniature golf course! Let's stop and play a game or two."

"And get a hot dog or two!" Shaggy says.

"Rum, rum!" Scooby adds, licking his lips.

Inside the miniature golf course, everybody grabs a putter and a ball. Fred picks the blue ball, Daphne picks the red one, Velma picks orange, and Shaggy picks green.

"Looks like you get the white ball, Scoob!" Shaggy says as Scooby grabs the white ball from the bucket.

The owner shakes her head. "You might have some trouble with that white ball," she tells him. "We've had quite a mystery around here with the white balls disappearing."

Scooby gulps. "Ruh-roh!"
"We'll keep an eye on that golf ball, Scooby," Velma says.
"Let's bring an extra, just in case," Fred adds.

At the first hole, Daphne steps up and takes her shot. "Nice shot!" Fred tells her. Then Fred, Velma, and Shaggy take their turns.

"You're up, Scoob!" Shaggy says. "If you hurry, we can hit the snack bar before the next hole."

Scooby swings his club. The ball bounces back and forth, this
ay and that, and finally bumps against a big wooden box before
rolls toward the hole.

"What a great shot!" Daphne shouts.

"That's a hole in, like, one!" Shaggy cheers, and the gang claps
the ball drops in.

Before Scooby can celebrate his great shot, the lid on the wooden box flips open. A big, scary shape jumps out of the box.

"Bwaaahhh!" it yells as it leaps toward the gang.

"Zoinks! Zombie!" shouts Shaggy.

"Rombie! Raggy, relp!" cries Scooby, who jumps into Shaggy's arms.

The zombie stops right in front of the gang. It waves a broken golf club, and its mouth hangs open.

"Bwaaahhh!"

Scooby shakes in Shaggy's arms. Shaggy has his eyes closed. Velma walks over and taps each of them. "Hey, guys, you can open your eyes," she tells them. "Your zombie isn't a monster. It's more of a wood-and-spring kind of zombie." She points to the large spring attached to its back. The gang can clearly see that the zombie is not real.

"Hey, it looks like this golf course has a scary theme. Look at the sign," Fred says. Everybody looks to where Fred is pointing. "We're playing at Mrs. Shadow's Spooky Miniature Golf." The other holes on the course have vampires, werewolves, and witches.

"See, guys," Daphne says. "There's nothing to be afraid of. None of the monsters are real. Let's keep playing!"

The rest of the gang finishes the first hole. "For a minute there, Scoob, I thought we were going to be zombie lunch," Shaggy says.

"Runch?" Scooby asks.

The gang picks up their golf balls. When Scooby looks for his, he cannot find it anywhere!

"That's what the owner was talking about," Fred realizes. "The white balls keep mysteriously disappearing. Good thing we brought an extra ball." Shaggy looks at the zombie suspiciously as Velma looks at the ground by the hole.

The gang walks over to the next hole.

"Hey, look, a pyramid!" Daphne shouts. "This hole will be fun!"

"Yeah, and there are some mummies, too," Shaggy gulps. "Doesn't sound like fun to me."

Everybody takes a shot. Their balls roll into the pyramid, through the tunnels, and out the side of the pyramid.

"Hey! Looks like everybody got a hole-in-one!" Fred says.
"Well, everybody but Scooby," Shaggy adds.
Scooby looks around, but another white ball has disappeared!

"First ball-stealing zombies, and now ball-stealing mummies! What next?" Shaggy cries.

Velma walks over to look at a feather on the ground. The rest of the gang talks about the disappearing balls.

"I'm telling you, the monsters are, like, real!" Shaggy says.

"Hey, look!" Fred shouts, pointing at a large figure lurking in the shadows behind the bushes.

"Zoinks! MORE monsters!" Shaggy yells.

The mysterious shape suddenly runs away from the hole.

"Hey, wait! Don't run!" Fred yells to the shadowy figure. He turns
to the gang. "Let's follow him! He went that way!" Fred, Daphne,
and Velma run after the mysterious figure.

"Well, Scoob, if the creepy shadow thing went *THAT* way," Shaggy
says, pointing to his left, "then I say we go *THIS* way," Shaggy says,
pointing to his right.

"Roh-kay, Raggy!" Scooby agrees. They take off toward another
hole—only to run right smack into the shadowy figure!

Fred, Daphne, and Velma run over and find Scooby and Shaggy standing near an old man who is wearing overalls.

"He's the creepy ball-stealer!" Shaggy says.

"No, no, I haven't been stealing them," the old man replies.

"Then why are you sneaking around, hiding in the shadows?" Daphne asks him.

"I'm the groundskeeper here. I've been trying to solve the mystery of why the white balls keep disappearing," he replies.

"He's right," Velma responds. "He hasn't been taking them. But I think I know who has." She holds up a couple of red feathers. "I found these at each spot where Scooby's ball disappeared."

Velma then points to a scarecrow on the next hole. On top of the scarecrow's hat is a bird's nest. A red bird flies near the nest, watching over some white eggs—and Scooby's white golf balls!

The groundskeeper shakes everybody's hands and thanks them. "I'm glad you kids solved this mystery. All along it's just been the little bird thinking the golf balls were her eggs."

The owner thanks them as well. "I'll just make sure that we don't use white balls anymore so the poor little bird doesn't get confused."

The gang smiles, but Scooby looks disappointed.